Enid Blyton's

MAGICAL TALES

The Lost Beads

and other stories

This is a Parragon Book

© Parragon 1997

13-17 Avonbridge Trading Estate,
Atlantic Road, Avonmouth, Bristol
Produced by The Templar Company plc,
Pippbrook Mill, London Road, Dorking,
Surrey RH4 1JE

Text copyright © Enid Blyton Ltd 1926-29

These stories were first published in Sunny Stories,
Teacher's Treasury, Two Years in the Infant School,
Read to Us, New Friends and Old and
The Daily Mail Annual.

Enid Blyton's signature mark is a registered
trademark of Enid Blyton Limited.

Edited by Caroline Repchuk and Dugald Steer

Designed by Mark Kingsley-Monks

Printed and bound in Italy

ISBN 0 7525 1704 X (Hardback)
ISBN 0 7525 2322 8 (Paperback)

Enid Blyton's

MAGICAL TALES

The Lost Beads

and other stories

PARRAGON

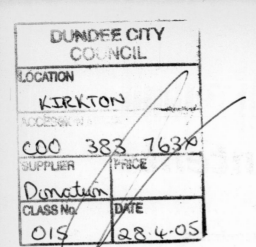

Contents

The Lost Beads

WHEN Angela, the big doll, lost her beads, she was really upset. She went crying to the toys, and they all listened to her story.

"I was walking in the garden, when my necklace suddenly broke," wept Angela. "And nearly all the beads rolled away down a hole. I put my hand down but I couldn't reach them. Look, I've only got two blue beads left of my lovely necklace."

"Don't cry, Angela," said the teddy bear. "We'll get Pip along. He's a Pixie who likes toys, you know – and Jinky too. They'll

think of something to get back
your beads!"

So Pip and Jinky were fetched
– and they thought of something
at once, of course!

"Down that hole, did you say?"
said Pip. "Now let me see – no
good asking the rabbit for help –
he'd scrape too big a hole and
scatter the beads everywhere. I
know – we'll get the mole. Go
and fetch him, Jinky."

Well, before long, a curious
little hillock of earth appeared in
the garden – and out of the tip of
it came the mole's sharp little
snout. "What would you like me
to do?" he asked.

Pip told him. "See that hole nearby, mole? Well, Angela's beads are there. Burrow a hole to them, will you, and collect them for her? You're always burrowing after beetles and grubs – why not burrow after beads for a change?"

"Right," said the mole, and disappeared underground again. They heard a lot of tunnelling going on, and then he popped up again. "Can't talk very well," he mumbled. "Got my mouth full of beads. Here they are!"

Angela was so pleased. She promised to tell him the very next time she saw a fat slug that would do for his dinner. "He's clever, isn't he?" she said to Pip. "And so are you! Thank you VERY much!"

The Seven Crosspatches

ONCE upon a time the seven Crosspatches caught a little pixie and made him their servant. How hard he had to work for them!

He didn't like the Crosspatches one bit because they were just like their name. They were cross old dames, and they made their money by selling spells and magic. They all lived together in a tiny little cottage which had two rooms.

There were seven chairs and a table in one room, and seven small beds in the other. Scurry, the pixie, was kept busy each day making the seven beds and polishing the seven chairs and doing all the cooking for the seven Crosspatches.

They were always cross with him and always told him off.

"You're one minute late with our dinner," one would say to him angrily.

"You've not dusted under my bed properly!" another would say to him.

"You've not wound up the clock!" the third would say. And the others would chime in, too, each taking their turn at scolding poor Scurry.

When spring cleaning time came he was quite tired out. He

had to wash all the curtains, all
the blankets, all the sheets and
all the tablecloths. He had to
whitewash the house outside and
inside. He had to sweep the two
chimneys. The Crosspatches kept
him hard at work from morning
till night.

But he didn't beat the carpets.
The magic spells that the old
dames were always making made
a terrible dust, and because it
was magic dust it made Scurry
sneeze and sneeze without
stopping and gave him the most
horrible magic cold.

"I'm not going to beat the
carpets!" he thought. "I shake

them every week and that's enough. Let's hope the old Crosspatches won't know they're not beaten."

But they did know, of course, and they were angry. "You'll take up each of our seven carpets tomorrow and you'll hang them on the line and beat them!" they said crossly.

"But I shall get a magic cold and sneeze all day long without stopping," said Scurry. "And that's very tiring."

"You can sneeze for a month for all we care!" cried the Crosspatches. "Now, make sure you see to it that every single speck of dust is beaten out of those carpets tomorrow!"

Well, the Crosspatches went out the next day because they didn't want to be in the middle of the carpet dust. Scurry took all the carpets and hung them on the line in a row. It made him feel very gloomy.

He began to beat one. His arm soon ached badly. Then an idea came to him. He would pretend he was slapping one of the Crosspatches! Everyone wanted to do that, because the seven old dames were mean, bad-tempered and selfish.

He fetched a piece of chalk. He

drew one of the Crosspatches on a carpet. He put a pointed hat on her head. He laughed, because really he had drawn her very well indeed!

"I think I'll draw a Crosspatch on each of the carpets!" he thought. "Yes, I will. Now this one is the Crosspatch that wears a two-pointed hat – and then I'll draw the one that wears a three-pointed hat – and then the one with one red rose in her bonnet, and the one with two, and the one with three – and last of all the Crosspatch that wears neither hat nor bonnet, but has her hair flying loose!"

So he drew a Crosspatch on each carpet. My, they did look funny. Then Scurry took up the carpet beater and began to slap the first Crosspatch hard! "That's for all your bad temper!" he panted, as he slapped a carpet with a drawing of a Crosspatch on it. "That's for your all your unkindness!"

Presently two or three of the village pixies came along and looked over the wall at what Scurry was doing.

"Goodness – wouldn't I like a slap at those horrid old Crosspatches!" said one. "The one with the two-pointed hat that boxed my ears for nothing the other day!"

Scurry was tired and out of breath. He looked round at the pixie and grinned.

"Well," he panted, "if you want a good old smack at the second Crosspatch, pay me a penny and you can have as many smacks as you like!"

The pixie hopped over the wall at once, and paid his penny. Then, with a grin, he took up the carpet-beater, and hit the carpet hard – the one with the drawing of the Crosspatch wearing the two-pointed hat.

"That's for boxing my ears!" he

panted. "And that's for scolding my little sister and frightening her so much!"

"I say! Let me have a turn, too!" cried the next pixie, scrambling over the wall. "I'd like to beat the last Crosspatch, the one who wears her hair loose. She lost her temper with me the other day and stamped all round my garden, trampling on my flowers!"

He paid a penny to Scurry, who was beginning to feel very pleased with himself. He sat well back on the wall, right out of the way of the dust. Soon other pixies came along, and gazed in delight at the two who were slapping away at the carpets on which were chalked the Crosspatches everyone disliked so much.

Pennies poured into Scurry's purse. One after another the pixies came and had a good slap at the hated Crosspatches. Bang, bang, bang, biff, biff, biff, slap, slap, slap!

"Take that, you horrible, nasty, unkind Crosspatch!"

"That's for cheating me out of a whole shilling the other day!"

"That's for selling me a bad spell that didn't work!"

"That's for making my hens

stop their laying!"

All day long the beating went on and soon there was not a single scrap of dust left in the carpets, not one scrap. It was wonderful.

Scurry's purse was quite full of money. He looked at it. He had never had so much money in his entire life!

When the night came, the pixies went home. They *were* pleased. They didn't hate the Crosspatches quite so much now that they had slapped at them on the carpets. They didn't like hating anyone. It was a nasty, horrible feeling. They all felt much better now!

The seven Crosspatches came home and went to bed. Next morning they dragged out the seven carpets to see if Scurry had beaten them well. There was not one speck of dust in any of them! But the funny thing was that Scurry wasn't sneezing as he usually did when he had beaten the carpets.

"How did you manage to beat the carpets so well?" asked the first Crosspatch, the one with the pointed hat.

"I didn't," said Scurry. "I got the pixies from the village to beat them for me. They even paid me for letting them beat your carpets!"

"Don't talk nonsense!" said the Crosspatch with one red rose in her bonnet. "Why should the pixies pay you for doing your work for you?"

"Well, you are sure to hear about it, so I suppose I'd better tell you myself," said Scurry. "I drew a picture of each of you on the carpets – and the pixies from the village were quite willing to pay me a penny each after that, to beat you on the carpets! They don't like you very much, as you can guess!"

"How dare you! How dare

you!" cried all the Crosspatches together. "We'll turn you into a black beetle!"

"You won't!" cried Scurry, running to the door, jingling his money. "I'm rich now! I'm running away! Goodbye and be careful, Crosspatches! It's unlucky to be hated as much as you are. Be careful!"

The Crosspatches couldn't catch him, because he ran so fast. They looked carefully at their seven carpets. Yes – they could quite well see the outline of the seven pictures that Scurry had drawn there.

"Dear me!" said the first

Crosspatch. "Fancy all the villagers paying to come and beat us on our carpets. Perhaps – perhaps we have been a bit too hard with the pixies. Perhaps we'd better be a little bit more careful now."

"Yes," said the second Crosspatch, "because if not they might come to our house and really beat us!"

So they were much nicer after that. As for Scurry, he was so pleased with himself for being able to draw such good pictures that he set himself up as a painter in the woods. In the winter he helps Jack Frost to decorate our window-panes at night. He does all the funny little twiddly bits. Look out for them, won't you!

Here Comes the Wizard!

ONCE there was a wizard who used to live in a cave on High-up Hill. But that was a very long time ago, so long that not one of the brownies who went up and down the hill could remember him.

But whenever they came back from the market one or other always said the same thing: "It's a good thing the Wizard of Woolamalooloo is gone! We've so many goods with us that he would have a good haul if he popped out of his cave and stopped us!"

Then they would all laugh, because nobody lived in the cave

now, certainly not a wizard.

The path to the market lay up the hill and down, and passed near the old cave. The brownies loved going to market each Friday and coming back with all the things they had bought for their wives and children.

One day a new brownie came to live in Whispering Wood with the others. His name was Smarty, and he certainly was smart. He got better bargains at the market than anyone else.

When he heard the story of the old wizard who once lived in the cave, he thought about it. The next time the brownies walked down the hill near the cave, bringing home their goods from the market, Smarty listened to hear the usual remark. It came!

"It's a good thing the Wizard of Woolamalooloo is gone. We've so many goods that he would have a good haul if he popped out of his cave and stopped us."

Then Smarty spoke in a very solemn voice. "The Wizard of Woolamalooloo has come to live not far from here. I knew him before I came – a most unpleasant fellow. And he told me that one day he might come back here, hide in his cave and pop out at us when we were coming back from market."

Everyone looked most alarmed. "I don't believe it," said Stouty, a burly, good-natured little brownie.

"Ho!" said Smarty, "you don't? Well, all I can say is this – that if ever any one of us yells out that he can see the wizard waiting for us, we'd better drop our goods and run down the hill for all we're worth."

"Stuff and nonsense!" said Stouty.

"I don't know," said little Peeko. "If the old wizard is about, and comes here, I think Smarty's idea is a good one. If we try to run away carrying our heavy goods, we'd soon be caught. Far better to drop our things and go!"

"Well spoken," said Smarty. "Well, I've warned you. We'll all keep watch the very next time, in case the wizard is around! I've a feeling he may be!"

Stouty looked at Smarty, and thought a lot. That wizard wouldn't come! Smarty was making it all up for some reason or other. What was the reason? Stouty thought he could guess!

Now, on the next market day, all the brownies except Stouty, went to market as usual, and back again. Smarty went, too, of course. They came back up the hill, and then went down the other side, keeping a sharp look-out for the wizard.

And suddenly Smarty's voice rang out loudly: "There he is! Behind those trees! I can see him lying in wait for us. Drop your things and run, brownies, run, run, RUN!"

The brownies shrieked and yelled. They dropped all the goods they had bought and ran down the hill at top speed.

All but Smarty. He waited till they were out of sight, then he laughed. He began to pick up the dropped goods, and stuff them into a big sack.

"How foolish they are!" he said. "They rush off and leave all their goods to me – and there isn't a wizard for miles around."

Then a deep voice spoke from the nearby cave and he nearly jumped out of his skin.

"Smarty! Come here! Bring those goods to me!"

Smarty went pale and jumped. Who was that? "Who are you?" he stammered.

"Well, you told the others," said the deep voice. "Who used to live here, Smarty? Why, the Wizard of Woolamalooloo! Bring those goods to me, Smarty – and all your own goods, too!"

Smarty wailed in fright. Oh, oh, to think the real wizard was there, after all! What a piece of bad luck. Shaking with fright, he took everything to the cave, and threw it down outside. He could not see inside because it was far too dark.

"Leave the goods there," said the deep voice. "And come inside, Smarty. Come inside and see what happens to nasty little brownies like you. Come inside, Smarty."

But Smarty didn't. He fled over the hill, back to the market, through the town there, and out to the land of Far-Off-and-Forgotten. Never would he go back to Whispering Wood again!

The wizard in the cave chuckled as he saw Smarty tearing away. He came out – and dear me, what was this? He was no wizard! He was just Stouty the brownie, not even dressed up! He picked up the sacks of goods and went down the hill to the town, laughing loudly.

The other brownies gathered round him eagerly. "Stouty – how did you get our goods? Oh, Stouty, did you see the wizard? Stouty, weren't you afraid?"

"No," said Stouty, with another laugh. "Why, that wizard lost all of his magic powers one day and had to go to work for my great-granny – and he's there still, digging her garden and weeding and watering for her all day long. The Wizard of Woolamalooloo indeed! We all call him Wooly for short and he really wouldn't hurt a fly!"

"You're better than any wizard, Stouty!" said his friends. "We guess Smarty won't come back here any more!"

He won't. He's much too afraid of the wizard who wasn't there!

Jimmy s Robin

IN Jimmy's garden lived a fine cock robin. You should have seen him! He had a beautiful red breast and the brightest black eyes, and he flew down beside Jimmy every time the little boy went to dig in his garden.

Jimmy gave the robin crumbs each day, and he often sang a little sweet song to Jimmy, and once, for just a moment, he flew on to Jimmy's head and stood there! Wasn't that friendly!

Then one day Jimmy was ill. He had to go to bed, and the little robin missed him badly. He hunted all over the garden for Jimmy, but he was nowhere to be seen. So the robin thought he would go and look in the house. Perhaps Jimmy was there!

He looked in all the windows – and at last he found Jimmy, lying in bed, looking very miserable, for the little boy was lonely. The robin flew in at the open window and then sat on the bottom of Jimmy's bed.

"Tweet, tweet, chirry, chirry, chee!" he sang. Jimmy opened his eyes and sat up in delight.

"Why it's my robin!" he said. "Oh, robin, how nice of you to come and find me! It's been so dull lying here in bed! Do come and see me every day!"

47

"Tweet, tweet, I will!" said the robin. He flew down on to Jimmy's blanket and sang a little song there and then he flew out of the window again. He had thought of such a good idea! He had a little wife and they were looking for a good place to build their nest. What fun it would be if they could find a place in Jimmy's bedroom! Jimmy was such a nice boy, and the little robin would like to build somewhere near his friend.

He found his wife and told her his good idea. Then together they flew back to Jimmy's bedroom and looked into every nook and corner to see if they could find a good place to put their nest.

"What about behind this bookcase by Jimmy's bed?" said the robin. "There is just room."

"Tweet, chirry chee!" said his wife. "Yes, that will be fine!"

So, for the next few days, Jimmy had a lovely time, watching the little robins build their nest in his bedroom! He didn't tell anyone, because he was afraid that Mother might say they were making a mess. He just lay and watched the little birds fly in and out – sometimes with a wisp of root, sometimes with two or three dead leaves, sometimes with a bit of moss.

One day the robin pecked a few hairs out of Jimmy's hairbrush! Jimmy did laugh! The hairs went into the nest too. Then the robin's wife sat down on her cosy nest behind the bookcase and laid four pretty, red-spotted eggs. Jimmy could just see them if he peeped behind the bookcase. It really was very exciting!

"I can't understand how it is that Jimmy is so good and happy, staying all this time in bed!" said Mummy to the doctor. "He is just as good as gold!"

Jimmy knew why he was so
happy and good. It was because
he had two friends living behind
his bookcase. But he wasn't
going to say a word!

One day the eggs hatched out
into tiny baby birds. The two
robins sang loudly for joy. Jimmy
sang for joy too! He was just as
pleased as the robins. He peeped
behind the bookcase and looked
at the baby birds each day.
Sometimes the two robins would
fly off to get food for them, and
Jimmy would look after them.
He promised the robin that he
would not let pussy come into
the room.

And then the little robins grew so big that it was time for them to fly away! And do you know, they all got out of the nest and flew about the room! Just imagine that! Jimmy laughed so loudly – and just at that moment his door opened and in came Mummy with the doctor!

"Well!" said Mummy, in surprise. "Wherever did all these birds come from?"

And then Jimmy had to tell about the nest and show Mummy and the doctor where it was built behind the bookcase. Mummy was so surprised!

"But I am very sad now," said

Jimmy, "because, you see, the babies are flying away and I won't see the robins any more. They will be about the garden, with their father and mother. It is time they flew out of this room."

"And it is time you flew out of this room too!" said the doctor, smiling. "It is lovely sunny weather and you are to lie out in the garden all day long now – so you will be able to see your robins all the time!"

Jimmy was so pleased – and now he and the robins are in the garden together, and Jimmy is nearly well again. He has six tame robins – isn't he lucky!

The Land of Golden Things

ONCE upon a time there was a king who was very poor. He hadn't even a palace to live in, and that made him very sad. He had a crown to wear, it is true, but it wasn't made of real gold, and it only had six precious stones in it.

He lived alone in a cottage with his little daughter Rosamunda. He had spent all his money in going to war with another country, and had lost the battle. His people were too poor to help him – so there he was, a king no better than a pauper.

His cottage was built in a lovely place looking out over the blue sea. He had one cow that gave him creamy white milk, three hens that laid him eggs every day, and an old servant woman who cooked nice, simple meals for him, grew fine vegetables in the little garden, and looked after Rosamunda.

The King was very unhappy. He longed for a palace, he longed for a treasure chest filled with gold, he longed for hundreds of servants, fine clothes and beautiful furniture. His little daughter grieved to see him so miserable, and tried to make him laugh and smile – but it was very difficult.

Rosamunda was happy. She knew she was a princess, but she was glad she didn't live in a palace. She liked to feed the three hens, and milk the gentle cow. She loved to paddle in the warm pools, and walk out on the windy hills.

Best of all she liked to work in the little garden that belonged to the cottage. She loved to grow bright flowers and pick them for the jugs and bowls indoors. She used to take big bunches of sweet-smelling roses to her father, and make him look at how lovely they were.

"Look, Daddy," she would say.

"Smell them. Aren't they beautiful?"

But the King wouldn't bother about them. If they had been made of silver or gold, he would have seized them eagerly – but they weren't.

One day in the summer-time he had a birthday. Rosamunda planned to give him a lovely present. She had a little rose-tree in a pot, one that she had grown all by herself, and she meant to give her father this.

She gave him a birthday hug, and then suddenly brought out the dear little tree. It was covered with tiny pink buds and blossoms, and was just like a fairy-tale tree. Rosamunda felt sure her father would love it.

But, do you know, he didn't even look at it properly! He just glanced at it, and said "Thank you, my dear," and nothing else at all. He didn't say, "Oh, what a lovely little tree! How I shall love to have it and look after it!" Rosamunda was dreadfully disappointed.

"Daddy, darling, you must be sure to water it every single morning before the sun gets hot," she said to him. "It is rather a delicate little tree, so please see that it gets enough to drink."

The King put it on the window-sill in his tiny bedroom, and then forgot all about it. He sat down and thought of the birthday he would have had if he had been a king with lots of money and a rich kingdom.

"I should have had a hundred guns fired off," he thought. "Then people would have come to my throne bringing me gorgeous presents. At night I would have given a grand party, and had kings and queens, princes and nobles for my guests. Wouldn't it have been fine!"

He made himself so miserable, grieving over this, that for quite a week he forgot to smile at Rosamunda. She was sad because she loved him. She felt sure, too, that he had forgotten to water the little tree she had given him.

One bright morning the King went for a walk through the fields that lay behind his cottage. As he went on his way, a stranger approached him. He was a fine looking youth, tall and strong.

"Can I help you?" asked the King, seeing that the stranger seemed to have lost his way.

"That would be kind of you," said the youth. "I want to get back to the place where I have left my carriage, and I cannot find the way. It was by a lovely little blue stream that ran through a wood."

"You have wandered for miles then," said the King. "I know the stream. Let me take you back myself. I am sorry I have no servant to guide you, but there is only the old woman in the cottage. I am a king, but have none of the things a king should have, as you can see – except for my crown."

"That is very good of you," said the stranger. So he and the King walked over the fields together, and after about two hours came to where the carriage had been left.

How the King stared when he saw it! It was made of pure gold, and shone in the sun so brightly that the King was dazzled when he looked at it.

There was a coachman there, clad in a golden livery, and eight footmen, all in gold breeches and coats of fine brocade.

"How rich you must be!" said the King enviously.

"Let me drive you to my kingdom, and you shall see it," said the strange youth. "It is supposed to be one of the most wonderful places in the world."

The King stepped into the carriage. The coachman flicked his golden whip, and the horses started forward. How fast they went! The King knew they must have some sort of magic in their blood for they went too fast for him to see anything out of the windows at all. Trees, houses and hedges flashed by in a long line.

At last the carriage stopped in front of a vast, golden palace. The King shut his eyes after giving it one glance for it was so dazzling. He went up the golden steps, feeling quite dazed.

The stranger gave him a wonderful meal served on golden

plates with an edging of diamonds. He drank from a golden goblet studded with red rubies and green emeralds. Servants clad in rich golden draperies stood in dozens around the golden hall. How the King envied all this richness!

"If only I had a little of your marvellous store of gold," he said to the stranger, "how happy I should be!"

"You shall have as much as my carriage will hold when it takes you home again," said the youth. "I have so much that I am glad to get rid of some of it."

After the meal the King went

to see the treasure-house. There were not only bags of gold there, and chests filled to the brim with golden bars, but also rare treasures. There was a golden apple that could make anyone who was ill feel better at once merely by holding it in his hand. There was a goblet set with sapphires which was always full of the rarest wine in the world, no matter how much was drunk from it.

The King looked at all these things longingly. Then he saw a beautiful mirror, and he picked it up to look at.

"That mirror will show you the

picture of anyone you think of," said the stranger. "Think of someone now, and take a look in the mirror."

The King at once thought of one of his old generals, and looked into the mirror. A picture came there, and he saw an old bent man working in a potato field. When the man stood up, the King saw that it was his old general.

"Dear, dear!" he said, sadly. "To think that my famous old general should be working in a potato field!"

Then he thought of the King who had defeated him, and

immediately a new picture came into the mirror. It showed a fat, ugly man sitting at a well-laden table. He wore a heavy crown, and he frowned at his Queen, who was sitting beside him. She was speaking sharply to him, and though the King could not hear what was being said, he knew that she was cross with his old enemy and was scolding him.

"Aha!" he said. "So my foe has grown fat, and his Queen leads a miserable life!"

Then he turned to the youth.

"This is a marvellous mirror," he said. "May I have it, for it would pass away many a weary hour for me?"

"What will you give me for it?" asked the youth. "It is a very valuable thing."

"I have so little that I can give," said the King. "Would you like a cow? Or a hen perhaps?"

The youth laughed.

"No," he said. "You shall give me whatever you see first tomorrow morning! As soon as you set eyes on it, it will vanish away to my kingdom. It will be amusing to see what comes!"

The King took away the mirror happily. He saw many bags of gold stowed away in the carriage that was to take him back to his cottage, and on the way home he made all kinds of plans.

"I shall build myself a fine house," he decided, "and get a new crown. Rosamunda shall have her first silken dress and a golden necklace."

It was late when he arrived back at the cottage. The footmen helped to dump all the bags of gold under the tree in the little garden, and then off went the golden carriage into the night.

The King was tired. He undressed and got into bed, thinking of the wonderful mirror.

"I shall look at the little rose-tree that Rosamunda gave me for my birthday," he thought. "That shall be the very first thing I set eyes on. It is about the only nice thing in this bedroom. I am sure the stranger will be pleased to see it arriving in his kingdom."

He fell asleep. When the early morning sun streamed into his room, he still slept. But Rosamunda was awake. She was out in the garden singing merrily. She looked up at her father's bedroom, and wondered if he was awake. She caught sight of the little rose-tree on his window-sill, and she saw that it was drooping.

"Poor little tree, it wants

water," she said. "I will steal into Daddy's room and water it before the sun gets hot."

She took a jug, filled it with water, and crept up to her father's room. She knocked, and then knocked again. When she got no answer, she opened the door, and peeped in. She saw the King lying fast asleep in bed, so she ran lightly across the floor to the window, and began to water the rose-tree.

At that moment the King awoke. He remembered that he meant to look at the tree first of all, so he opened his eyes and glanced across at the window where the tree stood.

But Rosamunda stood there in front of it, watering it! The King saw her immediately – and then she vanished before his eyes!

"Oh!" said the King, in horror. He sat up, and rubbed his eyes. Then he looked again. There stood the little tree, and there on the floor lay the jug that his little daughter had been using. But Rosamunda was quite gone.

"She's vanished to the land of golden things!" groaned the King. "Oh, what shall I do?"

He got up and went to the window. Then he saw all the bags of gold lying under the tree in the garden, and in delight he rubbed his hands and laughed. He forgot all about Rosamunda, and dressed quickly in order to go and run his hands through the golden coins.

He thought no more of his little girl all that day till the old servant came to him in distress and said that she could not find Rosamunda anywhere.

Then the King remembered what had happened, and told the servant about it.

"Oh, oh, oh!" she sobbed, wringing her hands. "To think of my little pet all alone in a strange land! Oh, you wicked man, to forget all about your little lamb like this! What is gold compared with Rosamunda's silken hair, merry eyes, and loving smile?"

The King suddenly felt miserable. How could he have forgotten his happy little daughter? He went red with shame, and turned away his head. But how could he get Rosamunda back? He did not know the way to the land of golden things.

All that week the King missed the little girl badly. He could remember Rosamunda's sweet smile and her loving voice. He could remember the feel of her warm hugs and kisses. He longed to hear the patter of her little feet. But instead of Rosamunda in the garden, he had bags and bags of gold.

Then he remembered the wonderful mirror he had brought back with him, and he looked into it. He thought of Rosamunda, and immediately the mirror showed him a picture of her.

She was standing in a garden, picking roses from a glittering bush. But alas for poor Rosamunda! The roses were golden, and had no smell, no softness, no beauty.

The King watched his little daughter in the mirror. He saw big tears streaming down her cheek as she held the hard rose in her hand. He knew how much she must miss her own little cottage garden, with its pretty, sweet-smelling flowers growing everywhere from seeds she herself had planted.

"Oh, if only I could get my little daughter back again, I would be happy here for the rest of my days!" he said. "I would willingly give back this gold and this marvellous mirror if I could have Rosamunda in their place! I have been a foolish man, always pining for riches when beside me I had Rosamunda, worth more than a hundred thousand bags of gold. How hard she tried to please me, how sweet she was, and how she loved me!"

The unhappy king walked out into the fields and wept loudly. Suddenly he saw the bright stranger again, and he ran up to him eagerly.

"Tell me about Rosamunda!" he cried. "Is she wanting me? Is she sad?"

"Very sad," said the stranger gravely. "Will you take her back, in exchange for the gold and the mirror, oh King?"

"Willingly, willingly!" cried the King with joy. "I am cured of my foolishness. I no longer wish for anything more than my little daughter. If I have her I am richer than any king in the whole world!"

"She is in my carriage over there," said the stranger with a smile. The King turned and saw the golden carriage standing in a narrow lane nearby. He scrambled through the hedge, tearing his clothes terribly, but he did not care one bit!

There was Rosamunda looking out of the carriage. When she saw her father she gave a shriek of delight, opened the door, and fell into his arms. How they hugged and kissed one another! How they laughed and cried! They quite forgot about the stranger.

By the time they remembered him, he was gone. Vanished too were the bags of gold, the mirror, and the wonderful golden carriage. But the King laughed to see them gone. He had got Rosamunda, and that was all he cared about.

"Daddy, you seem different," said Rosamunda. "I believe you love me after all. We will be happy together now, won't we?"

"We will!" said the King. "You and I will work in the garden together, and go for walks together, row on the sea together, and won't we be happy, Rosamunda?"

"Throw your crown away, Daddy!" cried the little girl. "Don't be a silly old king with no money and lots of frowns and sighs. Be a nice Daddy, and smile and laugh every day!"

She took the crown from the King's head, and threw it into a nettle-bed! The King looked horrified at first – but soon he laughed. And never again did he want to be rich, for he knew that was foolishness. Now he and Rosamunda are as happy as the day is long.

As for the little rose-tree she gave him for his birthday, they planted it out in the garden. It has climbed all over the cottage now, and if you happen to visit them in the summer-time, you will see how lovely it is.

The Dog Without a Collar

BOBBO was a fat little puppy, and he belonged to Rosie, who loved him very much. When he was six months old Daddy said that he must now have a collar with his name and address on it. So Rosie took him to a pet shop with Mummy, and together they chose a beautiful red collar for him.

"We will have his name and address on a little silver tag, to hang on to his collar," said Mummy. The shop assistant showed Mummy and Rosie some round, silver tags, and they chose the one they liked best.

"Please put Bobbo's name and

address on by the time we come back from our walk," Mummy said. Sure enough, when they called at the shop again the collar was ready, with the little round tag hanging on it, and neatly printed on the medal was:

Bobbo,
c/o Rosie Brown,
High Street, Benton.

"Oh, doesn't it look nice!" said Rosie, pleased. "Won't Bobbo be proud to have a brand new collar of his own!"

But do you know, Bobbo wasn't at all proud or pleased!

When Rosie buckled it round his neck he wriggled and struggled to get away, and was as naughty as could be.

"Oh, Bobbo!" said Rosie, disappointed. "Why don't you like your lovely red collar? All dogs wear them, and see, I have had your name and address put on this little round tag for you."

But Bobbo yelped and barked crossly, and when at last the collar was on he did his best to bite it – but of course he couldn't, because it was round his neck.

"You shall only wear it when we go out, till you get used to it, if it bothers you," said Rosie, kindly. So each night she took it off and popped it into a drawer.

One night she forgot to put it into the drawer. She left it on the chair instead. Bobbo saw it, and when he was alone, he went up to it and snarled.

"You horrid thing!" he said. "You nasty collar! I've a good mind to chew you!"

He took it into his mouth and bit it hard. Then he heard someone coming, and he quickly ran into the kitchen with the collar and dropped it into a bucket under the sink. Wasn't it naughty of him? He thought no one would find it there.

Next morning Rosie looked
everywhere for Bobbo's collar,
but it was nowhere to be seen.
Bobbo lay in his basket and said
nothing. He was feeling very
pleased to think that he wouldn't
be able to wear that horrid collar
all day.

Daddy found it when he took
the bucket to fill with water.

"Rosie, Rosie!" he cried.
"Here is Bobbo's collar. It was in
my bucket."

"Well, however could it have
got there?" said Rosie in
surprise. "Bobbo, come here! I'll
put it on your neck!"

Bobbo was angry. He made up

his mind to bury his collar in the garden, where no one could find it, the very next time he could get hold of it.

Two days later, as he was playing about in the garden, his collar came off all by itself! Rosie hadn't buckled it on properly, and it had come undone. Bobbo was delighted.

"Wuff!" he barked. "Now I'll bury it deep down in the earth, where no one will ever be able to find it again!"

He dug a big hole, dropped the collar down into it, and then covered it over with earth. How pleased he was!

"Now I'll go out for a walk by myself without a collar," he thought. "How jealous all the other dogs will be to see me without a collar!"

Off he went. He walked down the street, with his head well up in the air, and when he met another dog, he wuffed loudly.

"Wuff!" he said. "Why do you bother to wear a collar? I don't!"

"You'll wish you did, sooner or later," said the dog, scornfully. "You're silly."

The next dog he met laughed at him.

"Only puppies don't wear collars," he said. "I suppose

you're a silly puppy still?"

Bobbo went on and on – and when he had gone a very long way indeed, and had turned his nose up at quite twenty dogs with collars, he thought it was time to go home again.

But oh my goodness me! He

didn't know the way back! He had been so busy making faces at the dogs he met that he hadn't noticed the way he had come. He felt very much afraid.

"Oh dear!" he said, looking all round. "I wonder which is the right way to go?"

He chose a road that looked like one he knew – but it was the wrong one, and soon poor Bobbo found himself farther still from his home. He yelped in fear, and wondered what he should do. He saw a garden gate standing open and he went into the garden to see if there was anything to eat there, for he really was getting very hungry.

Suddenly he heard an angry voice shouting at him.

"You bad dog! What are you doing in my garden? No dogs are allowed here. Go away! Look what a mess you've made of my wallflowers, scraping up the earth like that!"

Bobbo looked up and saw an old woman shaking her fist at him angrily. He forgot where the gate was and tore off towards the house. He ran into the hall, and the old woman ran after him.

"Come out! Come out!" she shouted, "Oh, look at your muddy paw marks all over my clean hall! You bad, naughty dog! Just wait till I see who you belong to, and then I'll tell your master just how very bad you've been!"

Bobbo felt himself caught, and he stood trembling to see what would happen. He felt the old woman's fingers round his neck, and then she said in surprise, "Why, you haven't got a collar on, so I can't see your name and address. I shall have to call a policeman and tell him you're a stray dog."

Oh, dear! Call a policeman! Poor Bobbo shook all over. He didn't want to go to prison, and he thought he might have to, for making a mess of the old lady's clean hall.

The old woman went into the garden and looked over the gate. She knew that a policeman came down her street about that time. She saw him and called to him. Bobbo saw him walk up to the gate and he tried to hide himself, but it wasn't a bit of use.

"There's a stray dog here, policeman," said the old woman. "He's got no collar on, and no name or address, and he's made a dreadful mess of my garden and hall. You'd better take him along to the police station."

"Very good, Madam," said the policeman, and he picked Bobbo up and carried him away. Poor Bobbo! How he shivered and shook with fright! He soon arrived at the police station, and another policeman looked at him sternly and wrote something down in a book.

"Why don't people put collars on their dogs with their names and addresses?" said the second policeman, crossly. "It's such a waste of time, having to keep dogs here."

Bobbo was put into a bare little room by himself. He was hungry and thirsty, but the policemen were far too busy to think about little dogs just then. So Bobbo lay down on the floor to see what would happen next.

Nothing happened. The policemen forgot all about him, and the evening came. It grew dark in the little bare room, and Bobbo was cold and frightened.

"Oh, if only I'd got my red collar on!" he whined. "Then the policemen would know my name and where I lived and they would take me home. But they don't know who I am, and Rosie doesn't know where to look for me, and I can't find my way home even if I could escape, which I can't. Oh, why was I silly enough to bury my beautiful collar? All dogs wear collars, they are nice things to have. I do want my collar again!"

Suddenly the telephone rang, making Bobbo jump terribly. He heard the policeman in the next room answering it, and his heart jumped for joy when he heard what was said.

"Hello, hello," said the policeman. "This is the police station. Yes, we do happen to have a stray dog here, a puppy. But he's got no collar on, so we couldn't take him home. Yes, he's black and white, and very fat.

Very well, Miss, I'll keep him till you come for him."

Bobbo guessed that Rosie must have telephoned the police station about him when he didn't come in for his tea. He was so glad to think that he wouldn't have to go to prison, but was going home instead, that he frisked round and round the little bare room for joy.

Soon the door opened – and in came Rosie and her Mummy! You should have seen Bobbo rush to them! He jumped into the air, he licked their hands, he barked for joy. And all the time he was trying to say, "I'm very sorry I hid my collar. I'll dig it up again and wear it tomorrow like a good dog!"

But Rosie and Mummy didn't understand what he was saying. They just kissed him and hugged him, and then carried him home. They gave him some hot bread and milk as soon as they were home, and then he curled up in his basket, and fell fast asleep, tired out after all his adventures.

Next morning when Rosie called him, he ran up to her.

"I've got to get some more money out of my money box to pay for a new collar for you," said Rosie. "I don't know where your other one is. You are costing me a lot of money, Bobbo dear, because I had to give the policeman five whole pounds for being so kind as to look after you when you were lost yesterday. I do wish you hadn't lost your collar. If you had had it on, you would have been brought home as soon as you were lost, instead of having to go to the police station!"

Bobbo listened with his head on one side. He felt very much ashamed of himself. He ran to the garden and dug quickly where he had buried his collar. Soon he had found it and he carried it in his mouth to Rosie, and put it down at her feet. She was surprised.

"Oh, Bobbo, you had buried it!" she said. "Well, you have had your punishment, so I won't scold you any more. But I hope you will be a good dog in future and wear your collar every day without making a fuss."

Bobbo let Rosie put it round his neck. Then he licked her hand, and barked.

"I'll be a good dog now and always wear my collar!" he said. He kept his word and Rosie never had to look for his collar ever again, because it was always round his neck, making him look very neat and smart.

What an adventure he had, didn't he!

A Quarrel in the Morning

ONE early morning, just as the sun was getting up, a long, fat worm wriggled over the grass to his hole. He had been out all night long, enjoying himself, and now he was tired and wanted to rest in the little round room that was at the end of his hole.

Suddenly he heard the tippitty-tip noise of bird feet on the grass. He wriggled even more quickly, for he knew that it was time for the early birds to be about! Then he heard the hoppitty-hop noise of a frog jumping, and he felt about for the edge of his hole.

"That's a frog leaping along!"

thought the worm in a fright. "Oh, dear, where has my hole gone to? I know it's somewhere about here!"

Then, there came the noise of scurrying feet, and the worm listened in alarm. "A hedgehog! A prickly hedgehog! My goodness me, what a lot of my enemies are about this morning!"

He felt a tug at his tail. That was the blackbird! He felt a nip at his waist. That was the hedgehog! He felt a sticky tongue at his head. That was the frog!

"Leave me alone, leave me

alone!" cried the worm.

But the blackbird, the hedgehog, and the frog took no notice of him at all. They glared at one another.

"This is my worm!" whistled the blackbird through his bright orange beak.

"Pardon me – mine, you mean!" croaked the frog, his eyes nearly starting out of his head with rage.

"My dear friends, you are both making a big mistake," said the hedgehog, bristling all over. "I smelt the worm first, long before either of you did."

"Ah, but it was me that saw

him first!" cried the frog.

"I spied him from the topmost branch of that tree," said the blackbird angrily. "He was wriggling along fast, trying to find his hole. I flew down at once. He is my breakfast, so you two must go away and leave him to me."

"I am going to make my breakfast of him," said the frog, and he flicked out his long, sticky tongue. It was fastened to the front of his mouth, instead of the back, so he could flick it out quite a long way. The worm was nearly lifted into the frog's wide mouth. He would have disappeared down the frog's throat if the hedgehog hadn't suddenly knocked the frog aside with his nose.

"I shall eat him," said the hedgehog, and he ran at the worm with his sharp muzzle. But the blackbird pecked him so hard that he drew back.

"Do you want to fight me?" he asked, all his prickles standing straight up. "I can tell you, Blackbird, it is no joke to fight a prickly hedgehog like me! No animal dares to do that!"

"Oh, fiddlesticks to you!" said the blackbird rudely. "I'm not going to fight you. I'm going to eat my worm. If you try any tricks on me I can easily spread my wings and fly off."

"And then I shall gobble up my worm," said the hedgehog.

"You two fight and settle it," said the frog hopefully. "I'll watch and tell you who wins."

"Yes, and eat the worm while we're fighting," said the hedgehog scornfully. "We are not quite as stupid as that, thank you very much."

"Look, here's a mouse," said the frog suddenly. "Let's ask him to be our judge."

So they called the tiny mouse, who came over most politely and bowed to all three.

"Listen," said the hedgehog. "We want you to settle something for us. We each think we ought to have that worm. But we can't decide which of us shall eat it. We would like you to do the judging."

"Well," said the mouse politely, scratching his left ear as he thought hard. "Well – it seems to me that it would be a good idea if you all ran a race for the worm. The blackbird mustn't fly, though. He must hop. The frog can hop too, and the hedgehog can run."

"What shall be the winning

post?" said the blackbird.

"The worm's hole is the winning post," said the mouse. "Now, all of you go to the wall right over there and wait for me to give you the signal. I shall say, 'One, two, three, go!' "

So they all went over to the wall. But when they got there, the hedgehog called loudly to the mouse, "Excuse me, Mouse! I can't see the hole! Couldn't you stick something in it, so that we can see it?"

The mouse looked all round for something, but could see nothing that would do.

The worm spoke to the mouse.

"May I help you?" he said. "I could, if you liked, stick myself in the hole, and stand up straight with half my body out of the hole, so that I look just like a winning post."

"That's a good idea, Worm" said the mouse.

So the worm slid into his hole, and stood halfway out of it, very straight and stiff, for all the world like a little winning post.

"Can you see now?" shouted the mouse.

"Yes!" called back the others.

"Then, one, two, three, GO!" shouted the mouse.

The frog leapt high. The

blackbird hopped for all he was worth. The hedgehog ran as if he moved by clockwork, all his four little legs working together. And they all arrived at the winning post at exactly the same moment!

"Who's won, who's won?" cried the frog.

"All of you," said the mouse. "You, Blackbird, can have the end of the worm; you the head, Frog; and you the middle, Hedgehog. Goodbye!"

He scurried off. The blackbird, the hedgehog, and the frog turned to the worm hole. But the worm was gone. He no longer stuck out stiff and straight. He had wriggled down to his little room and was coiled up there, laughing to himself.

"Come up, worm!" shouted the frog, in a rage.

"I want the middle of you!" cried the hedgehog.

"And I want my share of you too!" cried the blackbird.

"Well, I'm sorry," called back the worm, "but I'm afraid I want the whole of me. Now go away. I'm sleepy."

The three looked at one another. "Why didn't we share him between us when we had the chance?" said the frog. "Well,

well, never mind. We'll do that next time we catch him."

But that worm is going to be very careful now – so I don't expect there will be a next time, do you?"

Mrs Tap-Tap-Tap

NOBODY knew what the little old lady's real name was. Everyone called her Mrs Tap-Tap-Tap, because she always used to tap with a stick as she walked along.

You see, she was blind, and she couldn't see, so she had to take a stick with her wherever she went, to tap along the pavement to find the kerb.

She was a nice, cheery old lady, and she often went out for walks by herself, but she could never cross the road unless somebody helped her, because she couldn't see if any cars were coming.

The children were very good to

her. As soon as any boy or girl saw Mrs Tap-Tap-Tap waiting at the kerb to cross the road, one of them would go up to her and take her arm. Then, as soon as the road was clear, they would take her safely across to the other side.

"Thank you, my dear," Mrs Tap-Tap-Tap would say, and off she would go on her way again, tap-tap-tapping with her stick.

One of the children who helped Mrs Tap-Tap-Tap a great deal was Johnny Watson. He always met her as he went home from afternoon school, and she often waited for him to help her across the road.

"Hello, Johnny!" she would say, as he came running up behind her. "I always know the sound of your feet."

"Hello, Mrs Tap-Tap-Tap!" Johnny would say. "Let me help you across the road. Wait a moment – there's a car. Now it's gone. We are safe."

This happened nearly every afternoon, and Johnny liked Mrs Tap-Tap-Tap very much, because she always had a joke for him.

Now one November afternoon a thick fog came down, and when Johnny came out from school he could hardly see the school gates.

At first he thought it was fun. Then he didn't – because he found that everywhere looked so very different, and he began to feel that he didn't know the way back home.

"It's this way," he said to himself, and he felt along the railings nearby. "I should come to a corner here."

But he didn't. There didn't seem to be a corner anywhere. He went back again, and tried to find where the school gates were, to start off home again. But he couldn't find the gates!

"This horrid fog makes everything as dark as night," said

Johnny, trying not to feel frightened. "Oh dear – wherever am I? I really don't know. I am quite lost."

He stood where he was for a little while, hoping that somebody would come along and he could ask them the way. But nobody came. Everyone was safe at home.

Johnny set off again, trying to read the names of the houses, so that he might know where he was. But it was too foggy even to do that.

At last he stood still again, thinking that he must be going even further away from home

instead of getting nearer. And
then he heard someone coming!

Tap-Tap-Tap! Tap-Tap-Tap!
That was the noise he heard.

"Goodness! It must be Mrs
Tap-Tap-Tap's stick!" said
Johnny. "Fancy her being out on
a dreadful day like this! I hope
she isn't lost too."

Presently Mrs Tap-Tap-Tap
came right by Johnny. He put out
his hand and stopped her.

Mrs Tap-Tap-Tap, are you lost
too?" he asked.

"Lost!" said the old lady in
surprise. "Of course not! Why
should I be?"

"Well, it's as dark as night

today, with this thick fog," said
Johnny.

"Little boy, it is always as dark
as night to me," said Mrs Tap-
Tap-Tap. "Blind people are
always in the dark, you know –
so what's a fog to me? I know my
way as well in a fog as I do in the
sunlight."

"Do you really?" said Johnny,
most surprised. "I never thought
of that."

"Ah, Johnny, you may be able
to get home all right in the
daylight, but I'm cleverer than
you in a fog." chuckled Mrs Tap-
Tap-Tap. "It seems to me,
Johnny, that I shall have to help

you today! Well, that will be a pleasant change! Come along with me. My house is just near here. We'll have a cup of tea, and then I will take you home."

Johnny slipped his hand under the old lady's arm and went along with her. She knew her way well. She tap-tapped with her stick, turned the right corners, and knew just which way to go. At last she came to a little house. She took the key from her pocket and opened the door. In they went.

A little plump lady came running up the hall. "I am glad to see you safe!" she cried.

"Safe as can be!" said Mrs Tap-Tap-Tap. "Now, Janet, please bring us tea and toast and some of my best shortbread. We have a visitor today – somebody who has helped me a lot at one time and another."

Soon Johnny and Mrs Tap-Tap-Tap were sitting down and eating a delicious tea. Then Mrs Tap-Tap-Tap put on her bonnet again and set off down the street with Johnny. It was still very foggy – but the old lady didn't mind about that. No – she could see as well in the dark as in the light!

It wasn't long before they came to Johnny's home. Johnny's

mother was so glad to see him. She hadn't worried about him really, because she had thought he was staying to tea at school as it was so foggy. She thanked Mrs Tap-Tap-Tap very kindly for bringing Johnny home safely.

"Oh, your Johnny has often done a good turn to me," said the old lady, smiling. "Now it's my turn to do a good turn to him. Goodbye, Johnny! You'll see me across the road safely tomorrow if it's fine, won't you?"

"Of course I will!" said Johnny. "I will be your eyes on a sunny day – and you can be mine on a foggy one!"

The Biscuit in the Chimney

ONE afternoon there was a party in the playroom. A lot of children came to tea with Jenny and William, and the toys sat and watched in delight.

"It's a birthday party," whispered Teddy to Sammy, the sailor doll. "William is eight today. Look at all the things they are having to eat."

"That's a birthday cake in the middle of the table," said the big doll, pointing to it.

"It isn't," said the toy dog. "It's got candles on. You don't put candles on cakes."

"You do on birthday cakes," said the big doll. "You're too

young to know, Toy Dog. Look –
they are lighting them!"

The toys watched in wonder.
What a beautiful cake, with eight
glowing candles in a ring! And
then, when it was cut, how
delicious it looked.

"I wish I could have a piece,"
whispered Teddy. "I've been
hungry all day, and now I feel
hungrier still."

"There might be some crumbs
on the carpet we could have,
when the children have gone,"
said the big doll.

The party went on till half past
six and then the children all said
"Thank you" and "Goodbye",

and went home.

Jenny and William danced back into the playroom with their mother.

"It was a lovely party!" said William. "Shall we clear up a bit now, Mummy?"

"Oh no – we'll leave it till tomorrow and then we can do it properly," said Mummy. "Now come downstairs and I'll read you both a story before it's time for bed."

So off they went and the toys were able to stand up and look round a bit. Were there any titbits left anywhere?

"I've got a bit of icing off the

cake!" cried the clockwork mouse in delight. "Look! Have a lick, anyone?"

"No – you have it yourself, Mouse," said the big doll. "It's only a small bit."

But the mouse broke it in half and gave a bit to the toy dog. It was delicious!

"I've got a bit of sponge cake – and it's got some jam on it!" shouted Sammy. "We can all share it."

So they each had a crumb and it really was very nice. Then Teddy found a large bit of egg sandwich and he shared that round, too.

Monkey had a good hunt round, but at first he didn't find anything. And then, quite a long way underneath the table, he saw something long and chocolaty lying on the carpet. Whatever could it be?

He went to see. Goodness! It was a whole chocolate finger biscuit that somebody had dropped. A whole one! Not even nibbled. Monkey could hardly believe his eyes.

Nobody was near him. He picked it up quickly and smelt it. Mmmm! Lovely! He licked it. Ooooh! Delicious! He looked round slyly at the others. If he shared it with them he would only have the tiniest little bit himself. If he didn't share it he could have the whole biscuit to himself. It would last him a very long time.

"The thing is," said Monkey to himself, "the thing is – where shall I hide it? It's so long. I can't put it into the brick box because the clockwork mouse often sleeps there and he'd smell it. I can't put it into the toy garage because one of the cars might run into it and break it. Where can I put it?"

He thought hard, sitting in a corner by the waste-paper

basket, hidden away from all of the other toys. Then he gave a little squeal.

"I know what I shall do! I'll climb up on the roof of the doll's house when all of the other toys are asleep – and I'll slip this long chocolate finger biscuit into the chimney. Nobody, nobody will ever guess it's there! I can go and get it out for a nibble whenever I want to."

So he waited till the toys were all asleep, and then he climbed up on the roof of the little doll's house. He slid the chocolate biscuit into the chimney. Yes, it went in beautifully. He pulled it out and had a nice long nibble at it. What a lovely chocolate biscuit it was!

A little mouse ran out of a hole in the playroom and startled Monkey. He dropped the biscuit down the chimney at once, and then scuttled down and ran over to the toy cupboard. Nobody must know where that biscuit was hidden!

Monkey was good at keeping secrets. He didn't tell anyone at all about the biscuit in the chimney. But he was so anxious to make sure that it was safe that he kept climbing up to the roof and looking down the chimney.

The toys were all very surprised at him.

"Monkey, why do you keep sitting on the roof and looking down the chimney?" asked Teddy. "That's the third time you've been up there this morning."

"Well – er – well, I'm just looking down to make sure it isn't blocked up," said Monkey, telling a fib. "You see, if the dolls ever wanted to light a fire and the chimney was blocked up in any way, it would smoke, and then their kitchen would become full of clouds of smoke and they wouldn't be able to breathe."

"But why should the chimney be blocked up?" asked the sailor doll, surprised. "It never has been. It's never smoked when the dolls have lit a fire. Of course smoke comes out of the chimney, but what you mean is that if it were blocked up the smoke would puff down into the fireplace and into the room. But why should it be?"

"I don't know," said Monkey. "But there's no harm in keeping an eye on it, is there?"

"Well, if you like sitting on roofs and staring down chimneys for a silly reason like that, we can't stop you," said the sailor doll. "Would you like somebody to help you to keep an eye on the chimney? There might be someone silly enough to."

"Oh, no. No, I can manage by myself," said Monkey, sliding down the roof and leaping to the ground. "I'm rather interested in chimneys, you know."

"I didn't know," said the sailor doll. "I've never thought that chimneys were so very interesting myself. Perhaps you are thinking of becoming a chimney-sweep, Monkey?"

Monkey didn't like being teased. He sat in a corner and sulked, waiting for a chance to go up on the roof of the doll's house again and have a nibble at the biscuit. If only the toys would go off and play in a corner somewhere! They did at last, and Monkey sprang up to the roof again. Could he manage to have just a little nibble?

But no – the big doll had seen him, and she called the others and pointed at Monkey. "He's up there again! He's chimney mad. Let's give him a chimney of his own when it's his birthday – one he can carry about with him!"

Now, the doll's house dolls got worried when they heard that Monkey was keeping an eye on

their chimney in case it got
blocked up.

"Why should he think that?"
they said. "Let's light a fire to
show him that it's quite alright.
He makes such a noise on the
roof, jumping up and down. It's
most disturbing."

So one night they lit a fire in
the fireplace of their dear little
house. The toys always loved to
see the fire in the doll's house lit,
it looked so cosy and friendly.
The teddy, the sailor doll and the
dolls went to peer in at the
window. They were too big to
walk in at the front door.

"It's alight," said Sammy. "I

can hear it crackling – and now, see, there are the flames!"

"It looks nice," said the big doll. "I feel quite warm just looking at it!"

"But see – it's beginning to smoke!" said the teddy bear, in alarm. "It really is! Clouds of smoke are pouring down the chimney into the kitchen! There must be something in the chimney! Monkey was right – it *is* blocked up!"

Monkey ran up.

"Oh, don't light a fire!" he begged, thinking of his lovely biscuit hidden in the chimney. The smoke would spoil it, he was sure. "Please don't light a fire!"

"Monkey, you were right – the chimney is blocked up," said Sammy.

Then one of the doll's house dolls gave a scream. "Help! Help! Something is streaming down the chimney and into the fireplace – oh, whatever is it?"

Well, you can guess what it was, of course! The heat from the fire had melted the chocolate, and it was running down the chimney into the fireplace in a warm, sticky river!

"It's running all over the floor. What is it?" screamed the dolls.

The clockwork mouse, who

could easily get in at the front door, ran in to help. He sniffed at the brown stream oozing down the chimney.

"Why – it's chocolate!" he said. "I know it is! I'll lick it and see!"

So he licked it and, of course, it was chocolate!

"But how could chocolate get into the chimney?" said the teddy bear, his nose pressed against the window outside. "What an extraordinary thing. Monkey, come here. Do you know anything about that chocolate?"

"He's gone as red as a tomato," said the big doll. "He knows all about it. Monkey – was it you who put it there?"

"Well," said Monkey, "well, you see – it's like this – er – well, this is what happened. You see..."

"What you really mean is that you found a chocolate or something on the floor and didn't want to share it and hid it down the chimney," said the big doll, who was very clever. "Mean old Monkey! And now the doll's house dolls have lit a fire to find out if the chimney is blocked or not – and your chocolate has melted. Ha, ha! You won't get it now."

"It was a chocolate finger biscuit," said Monkey mournfully. "It went down the chimney nicely. I wished I'd shared it out now!"

"Well, the clockwork mouse and all the toy animals from the farm can lick it up," said Sammy. "It serves you right. You won't even get a nibble. And I don't really feel I want to talk to you for quite a long while, Monkey."

The farm animals and the clockwork mouse were delighted. What a feast! The big toys watched them through the doll's house windows. All except Monkey, and he went and sat himself down with his face in a corner.

"Look – he's put himself in a corner," said Sammy with a giggle.

"Good thing, too!" said Teddy, "I'd have put him there myself if I'd thought of it."

They forgave Monkey after a while, but whenever it seemed as if he was going to be a bit mean again, they all began to talk loudly about chimneys. Then Monkey went red and stopped being selfish.

As for the biscuit part of the chocolate, that didn't melt, of course. It stayed in the chimney for quite a long while and then one day a real little mouse came into the playroom and sniffed it out and ate it.

Santa Makes
A Mistake

HAVE you ever heard the story of the night Santa Claus got stuck in the chimney? If you haven't, I really must tell it to you.

Not so very many years ago two children, Jane and George, lived with their Aunt Sarah and their Uncle Peter. Aunt Sarah looked after them very well, but as she didn't believe in fairies, or Santa Claus, she wasn't as nice as she might have been.

Jane and George believed in all those people, of course, and most of all in Santa Claus. They believed in him, because before their Mummy and Daddy had gone away to India, Santa Claus had brought them presents each Christmas.

"All nonsense!" said Aunt Sarah crossly. "All nonsense! What would you like me to give you for Christmas?"

"I'd like soldiers," said George.

"And I'd love a book of fairy tales!" said Jane.

"Soldiers are silly toys," said Aunt Sarah, "and as for fairy tales! Well! Just a pack of old nonsense! I shall give George a pair of nice warm gloves, and you a work basket, Jane. It's time you learnt to sew."

Now, George hated wearing

gloves and Jane hated sewing. Still they were much too polite to say so, and just said "Thank you very much, Aunt Sarah," and ran out to play.

"Let's write a note to Santa Claus," said Jane suddenly. He always used to bring us what we asked for, George!"

"Yes, let's!" said George.

So the children sat down and wrote a letter. This is what they said:

"DEAR SANTA CLAUS,
We hope you are well. Please do bring us a box of soldiers, and a book of fairy tales, if you have

some spare.
   With love from
   Jane and George."

   "Now let's put it up the
chimney," said Jane.
   The two children ran up to
their bedroom and poked the
letter as far up the chimney as
they could reach. They didn't say
anything to Aunt Sarah about it,
but just waited patiently for
Christmas to come.
   Now, I don't know whether you
know it, but Santa Claus is rather
fat, he has to make himself very
small in order to get down some
of our narrow chimneys. He can

do this easily by magic. He travels with a small fairy who always peeps down the chimneys first to see whether his big master can get down without making himself smaller. Then, while Santa Claus goes down to fill the stockings, the fairy holds the reindeer steady.

Well, on Christmas Eve Santa Claus arrived on the roof of Aunt Sarah's house. The small fairy jumped down, and peeped into the chimney leading to Jane and George's room. It was a nice big one. So Santa took his sack, stepped down from his sledge, and went up to the chimney-pot.

He swung his legs over it, and down he went.

But what do you think!

He had made a mistake, and slipped down the wrong one! He had got into the chimney that led to the dining-room where Aunt Sarah sat! And dear, oh dear! That chimney was terribly small! Santa Claus puffed and blew, and blew and puffed, and at last managed to squeeze himself down as far as the grate. Fortunately the fire had just gone out.

But Santa couldn't get out into the room! There he stuck, feeling very uncomfortable and very,

very annoyed.

And, oh dear me! Aunt Sarah was dreadfully frightened. She was just going up to bed, when she suddenly heard a noise in the chimney, and saw two fat legs appearing above the big grate. She thought it was a burglar.

"Help! Help!" she cried. "It's a burglar!" and ran straight out of the room.

Uncle Peter had gone to bed and was fast asleep. Only Jane and George were awake, wondering if Santa Claus would come that night. When they heard Aunt Sarah calling, they jumped out of bed, and quickly rushed downstairs to help her.

No one was in the dining room. Aunt Sarah was upstairs trying to wake Uncle Peter. Suddenly Jane pointed to the fireplace.

"Look, George! Look!" she said excitedly. "It's Santa Claus, but he's coming down the wrong chimney!"

Then a big voice came down the chimney and said:

"Is that you children? Give my legs a good pull and get me out of this chimney before your Aunt comes back, will you?"

So, the two children ran to the fireplace, caught hold of Santa Claus' big boots and PULLED and PULLED.

Then slither-slither-crash!
Down came Santa Claus and sat
panting on the hearthrug.

"Thank you! Thank you!" he
said. "Quick! Show me your
bedroom before anyone comes!"

Jane and George took him up
quickly just before Aunt Sarah
and Uncle Peter came running
down the passage.

"I made a mistake over the
chimney," whispered Santa
Claus. "Very silly of me! I'm
much obliged to you for helping
me out. I've brought you your
soldiers and fairy tales. But you
can choose anything else you like

for a Christmas present too, for being so kind to me. What would you like?"

"Can we choose anything in the world?"

"Yes, anything but only be quick!" answered Santa Claus.

"Then, please, please, PLEASE, send us Mummy and Daddy home soon!" begged Jane and George together.

"All right, I will!" smiled Santa Claus. "Get into bed, I am going out of your chimney now. Goodbye!"

Aunt Sarah couldn't think where her burglar had gone, and Uncle Peter thought she must have dreamed him!

When Jane and George showed her their soldiers and fairy tales next morning, she could hardly believe her eyes. They told her all about Santa Claus' visit and how he had come down the wrong chimney. "Dear, dear, dear! You don't say so!" she said. "Well, if he does send Mummy and Daddy back home soon, I will believe in him!"

And what do you think?

Mummy and Daddy suddenly walked up the garden path, just in time for the Christmas dinner! Did you ever hear of such a strange thing?

"Three cheers for Santa Claus!" said Jane and George.

And I really think he deserved them, don't you?

Grandpa's
Conker Tree

"LET'S go and see Grandpa today, and ask him if his conker tree has thrown down the rest of its conkers for us," said Peter to Joan.

So off they went. Grandpa always saw a great deal of the children in the autumn, because they did so like picking up the satiny, brown conkers that fell from his chestnut tree.

"Aren't they lovely, Grandpa?" said Joan. "And I do like their prickly cases. Grandpa, why does the conker tree put its conkers into such prickly, green cases?"

"Well, my dear, it doesn't want its precious brown conkers eaten,

that's why" said Grandpa.
"Prickles always stop birds or
animals from eating anything.
But, as soon as the conker is
ripe, and ready to root itself and
grow, then down comes the case,
it splits into three, and out rolls
the conker!"

"Grandpa, why did you plant
your conker tree in such a funny
place?" asked Peter. "It's
growing so near the wall of this
shed that it touches it all the way
up to the top."

"Well, you see – I didn't know I
had planted it!" said Grandpa.

"What do you mean?" asked
Joan, puzzled.

"I'll tell you about it," said Grandpa. "You know, I used to play conkers when I was a boy, just like you do. I used to choose a fine big conker, that I thought would be the conqueror of every other boy's chestnut – and we used to hang them on strings, and hold them out for one another to hit in turn."

"Yes – we like doing that," said Peter. "I've got a conker from your tree that is a forty-fiver, Grandpa! It has smashed forty-five other conkers belonging to the boys at my school."

"Well," said Grandpa. "I once had a wonderful conker, fat and solid and strong. I put a string through it, and then I set out to make it conquer every other boy's conker."

"And did it?"

"It became a one hundred-and-sixer!" said Grandpa. "What do you think of that? And then one day I was striking another boy's conker, and my hundred and sixer flew off the string, shot high in the air – and disappeared!"

"Didn't you find it again?" asked Joan.

"Yes, but not until the spring!" said Grandpa. "Then I found that my hundred-and-sixer had fallen just behind the shed there

– and had lain in the wet grass, put out roots and a shoot – and grown into a beautiful little chestnut tree!"

"Oh, do conkers really grow into chestnut trees?" said Peter, surprised. "Grandpa – suppose I planted my forty-fiver?"

"Try it and see!" said Grandpa. "Maybe you will get a fine big chestnut tree, which will throw down conkers for your grandchildren, as mine does for me! That would be fun."

So Peter is going to plant his conker and see what happens. Have you got one you can plant as well?

The Rabbit that Lost its Squeak

ONCE upon a time there was a blue rabbit with a red ribbon round his neck. He lived on a little chair in the dining-room, and belonged to Mollie. She loved him very much, especially because he had a lovely squeak when she pressed him hard in the middle.

You should have heard him! "Eeeeee!" he went, just like that. "Eeeeee!" He sounded so alive, and Mollie really thought he was the nicest animal she had. The bear could make a deep growl and her best doll could say "Mama!" in a funny little voice when she was turned upside-down –

but the rabbit's squeak was much more real than either the bear's growl or the doll's voice.

One day the rabbit rolled off his chair onto the floor. He lay there on the carpet and nobody saw him. So when Auntie Maud came into the dining-room, she trod on him, right on his little blue middle. He said "Eeeee-Eeeeeeeee-Eeeee!" all the time he was trodden on, and Auntie Maud nearly jumped out of her shoes with fright.

She looked down and saw the rabbit lying there.

"Dear me, I've trodden on Mollie's rabbit!" she said. She

picked him up and put him back on his chair. But do you know, his squeak was broken! Yes, quite broken – for when Mollie came in from her walk and picked him up, he wouldn't squeak, no matter how hard the little girl pressed his middle.

She put the rabbit down again, disappointed.

"He won't talk to me, Mummy," she said. "He's lost his squeak. I don't want him if he doesn't squeak. I'll give him away to the milkman's little girl tomorrow."

Well, when the blue rabbit heard that, he was terribly upset.

It would be dreadful to leave Mollie and go to live with someone else! Why, another child might pull his ears off, or twist his tail. Oh, dear, he really *must* stay with Mollie!

So that night he got down from his chair and went to look for a new squeak. He knew that mice squeaked and he knew that bats squeaked. So he thought he could go and ask one of them to give him a squeak, then Mollie would be pleased and would decide to keep him instead of giving him away.

He soon met a little brown mouse, hurrying along to pick up

some of the crumbs under the
dining-room table. "Hey,
Mouse!" called the blue rabbit.
"Eeeee!" squeaked the mouse in
a fright, trying to scuttle away
down a hole.

The blue rabbit caught him by
the tail and pulled him gently
back up again.

"Don't be afraid," he said. "I
just want to ask you something.
Could you let me have your
squeak? I'll give you the pretty
red ribbon that is round my neck,
if you will."

"Eeeeee!" squeaked the
mouse, still frightened. "Of
course I won't let you have my

squeak! I want it myself, don't I?
How am I going to talk to my
family if I let you have my
squeak? Don't be silly! Let my
tail go, or I'll bite you! Eeeeee!"

The blue rabbit sighed and let
the mouse go.

"What a pity!" he said to
himself. "That was a fine squeak,
and would just have suited me."

He went on again, and walked
out of a door into the garden. It
wasn't long before a little black
bat whisked round his head,
catching a beetle that was flying
by. The rabbit caught hold of the
bat's wing and held it gently.

"Eeeeeeeee!" squeaked the

bat, in a fright. "What are you doing? Let go!"

"Listen, Bat," said the rabbit. "I do so want a squeak, because I've lost mine. Let me have yours, and you shall have the red ribbon that is round my neck."

"Eeeee!" squeaked the bat, struggling to get free. "I don't want red ribbons! I don't want to give you my squeak! I'm frightened! Let me go or I will nibble your ear! Eeee!"

The blue rabbit let the bat go.

"I'm very unlucky!" said the rabbit, sadly. "I can't seem to get a squeak from anywhere. Hello, who's that?"

"It's only me, the cat," said a soft purring voice. "What are you doing out of doors at this time of the night, Blue Rabbit?"

The rabbit and the cat were great friends and often shared a chair, cuddling up to one another on cold nights.

The rabbit told the cat all about how he had lost his squeak and was trying to get another one, in case Mollie should give him away.

"I suppose you haven't a squeak you could let me have?" he asked the cat.

"No, I've only mews and purrs and hisses," said Puss. "But I tell you what has got a very fine squeak indeed, Rabbit – and that's the old gate at the end of the garden."

"Ooh, what a good idea of yours!" said the rabbit, and he ran down the garden path to the old gate.

"Gate!" he cried. "Have you a squeak you don't want?"

"Eeeeee-eee!" said the gate, as it swung in the wind. "Yes, I have a squeak. It is a perfect nuisance, because no gate should have a squeak. Gates should open and shut in silence. Eeeeee-eee!"

"It's a wonderful squeak!" said the rabbit, in delight. "Do give it to me, Gate. You see, I've lost my squeak!"

"I'd be delighted to, if only you'd give me a nice drink of oil, just where my hinges join me to the gate-post," said the gate. "Eeeeee-eee!"

"The oilcan is in the woodshed!" said the cat, quite excited. "I'll fetch it, Rabbit. I know just where it is ."

Off she went and came bank in a moment with a little oilcan.

"Eeeeee-eee!" said the gate, squeaking loudly as it swung open. "Pour the oil on my hinges, and you, Rabbit, climb up and sit tight on me, thinking of squeaks all the time. I will wish my squeak into your little blue middle."

The cat poured the oil on the gate's hinges, whilst the blue rabbit sat tight and thought of all the squeaks he had ever heard.

"There!" said the cat, putting down the oilcan. "How do you feel, Gate?"

"Fine!" said the gate, swinging to and fro quite silently. "Listen! My squeak has gone! I don't squeak any more! Have you got my squeak, Rabbit?"

"Eeeeeeeeee-Eee!" squeaked the blue rabbit suddenly, and fell off the gate in surprise and delight. "Yes, I've got your squeak! You've wished it into me! Oh, thank you, thank you! Eeeeeeeeee-eee!"

Back he went to the dining-room with the cat, and they both curled up together on the same chair and fell happily asleep. And in the morning along came Mollie to take the rabbit to give to the milkman's little girl.

She picked him up and pressed his middle. At once he squeaked very loudly indeed.

"Eeeeeeeeeee-eee!" he said. Mollie stared at him in delight.

"Mummy!" she cried. "Rabbit's got his squeak again – but it's a much better squeak! Do you know, it sounds just like the old garden gate when it squeaks in the wind! Isn't it funny! I shan't give Rabbit away now that he can squeak. I shall keep him. He has a most beautiful voice now."

How glad the blue rabbit was! He sank back on his chair and said: "Eeeeeeeeee-eee!" as loudly as he could. You should have heard him!